THE BIRD CAN 87 SAY MANY WORDS

KNOWLEDGE BOOKS

MASTERY DECODABLES

Tas is happy to get water for the bird.

The bird is happy to gulp water.

The bird is happy to stop.

The bird can speak.

The bird can say, Bec, Bec, Bec.

The bird can say, Bec bird, Bec bird, Bec, Bec, Bec.

Bec

Bec

Bec

Bec

bird

Bec

bird

Bec

Bec

Bec

Tas is with Bec the bird.

Bec can clap tired wings.

Bec can stop the long hot trip.

Bec is happy with Tas.

Tas and Bec can go to sleep.

Tas and Bec can go to sleep on the mat.

Tas likes Bec.

Bec likes to speak.

Bec can say, wet, wet, wet, sip, sip, sip.

Bec can stop with Tas.

wet

wet

wet

sip

sip

sip

16

Bec can stop with big Ted panda.

Bec can stop with Babbit
the rabbit.

Bec can drink water with Tas.

Bec is happy.